The Adventures of Stanley Kane

The Adventures of Stanley Kane

STAN J. GOLDBERG
&
VICTORIA CHESS

Harcourt Brace Jovanovich, Inc., New York

To my teachers

Printed in the United States of America
First edition
B C D E F G H I J

Library of Congress Cataloging in Publication Data: Goldberg, Stan J. The adventures of Stanley Kane. SUMMARY: Five brief episodes in which Stanley Kane and his friends, the dog, pig, and two cats, explore the use of their senses. [1. Senses and sensation—Fiction] I. Chess, Victoria, joint author. II. Title.
PZ7.G5644Ad [E] 73-75320 ISBN 0-15-201599-X

Book One

Stanley Kane lived in a big purple house. He had a dog, a pig, and two cats. One day he heard a knock at the door.

"Who is it?" he yelled. But there was no answer. The knock kept knocking.

The pig looked at the dog. The cats looked at each other, and Stanley Kane looked at the door, which was knocking.

"Let me in!" yelled the knock.

"Are you a good knock or a bad knock?" asked Stanley.

"I'm neither good nor bad—I'm just a knock," answered the knock, "and if you don't let me in soon, I won't even be a knock."

The cat looked at the pig, and the other cat looked at the dog, and

they all wiggled their tails. Stanley wished for just a moment that he had a tail to wiggle.

"You see," the knock went on, "when a knock is not answered, it stops knocking, and a knock that isn't knocking is no longer a knock."

Stanley was very confused and was getting a little annoyed at all this talk.

"What then is a knock when it stops knocking?" asked Stanley.

"I'll show you," said the knock.

The knock stopped. The purple house grew quiet. Stanley could hear the rain falling outside. The two cats went to sleep. The pig and the dog went to the kitchen to eat some chocolate cake, and Stanley Kane stood by the window wondering where the knock went.

Book Two

Stanley Kane looked out of his bedroom window. Night was coming across the sky like a big broom sweeping the last twinkles of day under a thick purple rug. The two cats winked at one another, and the dog and the pig sniffed the fresh night air. The moon looked down at the purple house, at the two cats winking, at the dog and the pig sniffing, and at Stanley Kane dreaming. The moon's light touched Stanley on the forehead. Stanley looked up.

"Hello," said the moon.

"Hello," answered Stanley. "I didn't know the moon could talk."

"Everything can talk," answered the moon.

The two cats paid no attention, and the dog and pig began to fidget.

"If everything can talk, then why can't I hear them?" asked Stanley.

"Because you don't listen," said the moon.

Lights began to flicker on in the distant village. The moon looked

down and stroked the fur of the two cats, patted the dog on the head, and tweaked the pig's tail.

"Thank you," said the cats.

"Thank you," said the dog.

"No thank you," said the pig.

"Moon, do you know any songs?" asked Stanley.

"No," replied the moon, "but I will teach you to find your own. Listen to the dog. Listen to the pig. Listen to the two cats. Listen

to the purple house, and listen to far-off village lights. Listen with your ears. Listen with your eyes. Listen with your nose, and listen with your heart."

Stanley listened and listened and listened. He listened with his ears. He listened with his eyes. He listened with his nose, and he listened with his heart. And Stanley began to sing. The two cats began to sing. The dog and the pig began to sing. The purple house began to sing, and the far-off village lights began to sing. Their songs danced in the light of the moon, and the moon listened.

Book Three

Stanley Kane was in his bed. He was very sleepy. The two cats were sleepy. The dog and the pig were sleepy.

"I wonder where you go when you go to sleep?" thought Stanley. "Do the cats, the dog, and the pig go to the same place?"

The grandfather clock in the hall struck nine. The two cats began to snore; the dog and the pig began to snore.

"Grumble rumble," went the first cat.
"Rumble grumble," went the second cat.
"Snoggle goggle," went the dog.
"Goggle snoggle," went the pig.
"Rumble grumble snoggle goggle-snoggle goggle rumble grumble."
"How can I ever get to sleep with all this noise?" thought Stanley, and he jumped out of bed and went to the kitchen to eat some chocolate cake. He cut a big slice and poured a glass of milk. As he sat and ate, a mouse came out of the wall.

"May I have some cake and milk, please?" asked the mouse.

"I thought mice ate cheese," said Stanley.

"I do, most of the time," said the mouse, "but there are times when only cake and milk will do."

"I know what you mean," said Stanley, and cut the mouse a mouse-sized portion of cake. "Do mice snore as loudly as two cats, a dog, and a pig?"

"Not quite so loud," answered the mouse, "for we are much smaller."

"If I move my bed in with the mice," thought Stanley, "then maybe I could get to sleep."

"Say, mouse, do you think I could move in with you?"

"That depends," said the mouse. "You see, my doorway is very small and you are very tall. That wouldn't do at all, that wouldn't do at all. What if you should fall and squish my brother Paul, or what if you should sneeze and blow away our cheese? And I ask you, if you please, if you come down with some disease and spread

it all among us, some green and creepy fungus, what are we to do, what are we to do?"

The mouse had lost all interest in the chocolate cake. He had even forgotten Stanley. All he heard was his own voice.

"Oh, what a wonderful voice," thought the mouse.

He picked up a tiny black cane, popped a straw hat on his head, and began to dance across the table. "Green and creepy fungus and blow away our cheese. What are we to do, what are we to do?"

"This is too much," thought Stanley. "A rhyming, dancing mouse. How could anyone get any sleep?"

Stanley got up and went up toward his room. Far below he could still hear the mouse singing. . . . "And squish my brother Paul, that wouldn't do at all, that wouldn't do at all."

Stanley climbed into bed and pulled up the covers. And before you could eat a mouse-sized portion of chocolate cake, he fell asleep.

Book Four

Stanley Kane sat on the porch of the purple house eating breakfast. The dog ate breakfast from a big blue bowl. The pig ate from a green heart-shaped bowl, and the two cats drank milk from a milky-shaped bowl.

"Breakfast is the best meal," thought Stanley.

"Every meal is the best meal," snooted the pig as he gobbled down the last crumbs of cream of wheat and brown sugar.

Stanley had finished and was watching the wind play with his crumpled napkin. He looked up and saw the wind play with the leaves of the trees. It played with the clouds. It played in ripples on the cats' milk, and it played wiggly-wiggly with the pig's tail.

"Wind," asked Stanley, "how can you play in so many places at once?"

The wind did not stop to answer. It picked up the napkin and carried it into the yard. It pulled a leaf from the tree and danced a hop with it in the air. It pushed at Stanley's back until he almost fell from his chair.

The dog began to fall asleep. The two cats began to fall asleep. The pig burped and said, "Excuse me."

"Wind," said Stanley, "have you a voice?"

"I have many voices," answered the wind.

The voice came from all places at once. It was very loud and at the same time very soft. It came from very far away, and at the same time its lips spoke as if they were next to Stanley's ear. He heard the voice in the floating of the clouds, in the wish-wish of the leaves, in the rumple-crumple of the napkin, in the wiggly-wiggly of the pig's tail.

"I wish I could play in so many places," said Stanley.

"You can," said the wind.

"But how?" asked Stanley.

"That is a mystery," said the wind.

"What is a mystery?" asked Stanley.

The wind whirled the napkin into the air and brought it down over the pig's eyes so he could not see.

"It's getting dark," thought the pig, and he went inside to see if supper was ready.

Stanley had waited a long time for the wind to answer. Then,

when he least expected it, he heard a voice.

"A mystery," said the wind, "is the smell of cinnamon toast when there is none. It is the taste of a cherry lollipop when the candy box is empty. It is the nearness of your friends, the cats, the dog, and the pig when they are far away playing. It is the blueness of the sky when outside it is raining."

"That's a strange answer," thought Stanley.

He picked up the big blue bowl, the green bowl, and the milky-shaped bowl and carried them inside to be washed.

Book Five

Stanley Kane sat quietly in his playroom. He and the pig were playing "Gribbledy-hop, gribbledy-hop, go to the market."

"It's your turn, pig," said Stanley.

The pig picked up a carrot in his mouth and tweaked it into the air. As it hit the floor, it spun around several times.

"I win, I win," said the pig, and he munched down the carrot. "Your turn," said the pig.

Stanley threw a fat red apple into the air. "Gribbledy-hop, gribbledy-hop, go to the market," yelled Stanley. The apple hit the floor with a thud.

"I win, I win," snorted the pig, and he munched away on the apple.

"Pig," said Stanley, "I have a question to ask you."

"Oh?" said the pig as he swallowed the last bits of apple core, seeds and all.

"Why is it," said Stanley, "that you always win?"

"That's easy," answered the pig. "It's the rules—the pig always wins."

"Oh, I understand," said Stanley. "And who makes up the rules?"

"I make up the rules for all the games I play," answered the pig.

At that moment the pig realized that he was getting thirsty and marched off to another corner of the playroom to play "Gizzle-gazzle-guzzle-the-milk" with the cats.

Stanley stood quietly and watched the afternoon sun as it fell through the five windows of the playroom. A ray of rose light fell

through the heart-shaped window. A ray of golden yellow light came through the sun-shaped window. A ray of green grassy light tumbled from the moon-shaped window. A ray of blue light fell through the watery-shaped window, and a ray of purple light pattered ever so quietly through the star-shaped window. The colored rays of light melted in wiggles across the playroom floor. The dog

hopped about, sniffing each color, but there was no smell. The pig tried to taste them.

"Ich," he snorted, for all he tasted was the floor.

Stanley looked at the light as it played about the room. The purple light made a cave on the wall and said, "Come in and explore me." The blue light formed a pool on the floor and said, "Come wiggle

your toes in me." The green light became a meadow and said, "Come feel my cool grass against your face." The yellow light rolled itself into a warm ball and said, "Come bake some mud pies by my side." But the rose light said nothing. It touched Stanley softly on the cheeks. It touched the two cats. It touched the dog and the pig. Stanley felt a strange warmth all over. He looked at the dog, at the two cats, and at the pig, and he spoke very softly to them.

"How nice it is to have such fine friends," whispered Stanley.

"How nice," said the two cats.
"How nice," said the dog.
"I win," said the pig.
"But this is no game," said Stanley.
"Then you mean I can't play?" said the pig.
"You don't need to play," said Stanley. "Just sit here quietly with your friends."
The pig sat quietly. Stanley, the dog, and the two cats sat quietly.

The last ray of evening fell through the heart-shaped window and danced a quick circle around the quiet friends.

"Good night," said the rose ray.

"Good night," said Stanley.

"Good night," said the dog.

"Good night," said the two cats.

"How nice," said the pig.